HIS UNKNOWN MYSTERY

'KIDNAP'

BY
Sheetal G

ISBN 978-93-5438-601-5

Published in India 2020 by Pencil

A brand of

One Point Six Technologies Pvt. Ltd.

123, Building J2, Shram Seva Premises,

Wadala Truck Terminal, Wadala (E)

Mumbai 400037, Maharashtra, INDIA

E connect@thepencilapp.com

W www.thepencilapp.com

Author biography

I'm An MBA finance graduate and I find my passion to write short stories, poems and novels

Contents

Chapter I

As the lights flickered and the shadows that grew

Footsteps I could hear in the dark haunted hill house, I paused for a moment and asked"Who are you?"

I looked around but none answered, surrounded by the strange silence, I asked again,"Who are you?"

A sudden chill ran through my nerves as my eyes widened, getting drawn to the person with burnt face draped in black, I screamed,"Go away !! Go away !!"And started running away

The person kept following me and it appeared in front of me as I stopped and said,"I haven't done anything to you and neither have I harmed you, please leave me alone ..."

"No ..., You've tortured me till my death, physically and mentally, cheated on me many times and yet I haven't said anything to you nor have I ever uttered anything to you. I waited long to take my revenge and today's my turn to take the revenge", said the person draped in black

"No ...No...No...You've misunderstood me, I haven't harmed you, to the extent that, I don't even know you", I said and I ran as fast as I could from the backside shortcut of the hill house through a small forest towards the mountains which was fencing the hill house. The shadow haunted me till the end of the small forest within the compound wall of the haunting hill house. I jumped off the compound wall and continued running deep into the forest until I was stopped by an old man who was grey-eyed

"Hold it !! Where are you running?"He stopped me asked as he looked deeply into my eyes

"I'm running to save my life, that house is haunted and I can't even stay here, so many weird and creepy things happen here, Run !!"I said to the old man as my breath shook heavily

The old man understood what I was trying to say and then he said,"I very well know that the house is haunted but now, you need to know something about this house and something's about your past"

"My past ??", I was shocked

"How I'm supposed to be connected with this house and what's my connection with this house that only you're aware of and I'm not ??, And how is my past supposed to be connected with this house ??", I questioned the old man looking very puzzled

Looking towards the haunting hill house from a distance, the old man said,"That house has a long history, A regretful past, That story which was not heard by many..but people ain't aware of what exactly happened behind those four walls"

"Then, how do they say that this house is haunted without even knowing exactly what went wrong and who were those people? Who are they? What happened, I need to know!"

"Then you need to stop questioning"

"I'll...", I agreed to the old man that I'll stop questioning him and a lot

We started walking in the forest where the old man resided, he seems to be knowing the whole history of the haunting hill house, the people, the events...etc, from the way he spoke initially in a very confident manner

I was sure that I'd get a few clues about the haunting hill house, as I wanted to write a horror story, but what happened was not as I had expected when we reach the older adult's house

HE TURNED OUT TO BE ONE OF THOSE BEST ARTISTS IN THE PAST !!

I was stunned seeing the painting hung on both sides of the walls and so many canvases painted very colourfully

"Seriously,!! Have you painted these masterpieces ?", I asked the old man

"Yes !! Very well !! I've made them all", the old man replied smilingly

I was so amazed to see the beautiful paintings hung on both sides of the wall,as the hall just looked like an exhibition

Seeing the paintings hung on both sides I said:"Wow !!, They're simply stunning !!"

"These are just a few to be named, Come along I've got to show you some more !!", The old man said as he took me upstairs to another room

We went upstairs to a private room where there were a lot of paintings being made of different themes, I was amazed after seeing these masterpieces, every painting had different meaning and emotion behind it

The older adult was quite happy as he showed me his collection of the paintings being made. He was explaining every emotion and intention behind every painting .

Every canvas was Colorfully filled , for except one which was covered with a white sheet of cloth,"why is that canvas covered with a sheet of cloth, Is it incomplete??", I asked

"No, it's not incomplete...But ..."

"But, what ??.."

The man removed the cloth slowly and what we saw was completely different. The painting was of a beautiful lady who looked similar to me , draped in red and sitting on a chaise lounge sofa with her lover beside her

"Doesn't she look little similar to me ?", I asked the old man as I carefully see the painting

"That's why I've got you here , to tell you about your past and answer all those questions you've asked me near the Haunting Hill House", the old man said

"Who am I ?, And how is it that you know everything about this house so perfectly ? And who is in this painting? Were you a witness for the events that took place in this house ? And this painting just looks like it's being made a few days ago , did you make this painting a few days ago ?", I started questioning the old man

"Again you started questioning ? , Keep calm , I'll answer everything" , the old man said as he drew his eyebrows a bit closer

"I made this painting k

"Wow !!, What a lovely couple are they?", I said as I smiled widely

"They look like they're made for each other , Who are they Sir ??", I asked the old man

A tear rolled down the old man's eye as he said"But that was ...."

The old painter's lips started shivering as he couldn't speak a word ahead

"That was what ??....., I said.

I see the color of painting combining up by itself into a very awkward expression of a person. In a moment or two, the man was suddenly pushed to the end of the room by a person that came out from the painting... loudly it roared at us as it came out of painting, I started moving backward and ran trying to save the older adult but the minute it looked into my eye ..it calmed down and everything became normal within few seconds

"Alas ..!! ...He disappeared..." , The old man said as he was panting and took a long breath

"Are you alright sir? , You were being pushed too hard by him"

"Yes, I'm alright...I'm fine .."

"Who was he? , And why did he attack you so harshly but the minute he saw me he just calmed down and moved away ..what's the connection between every one of us?"

Seeing the anxiety-filled in my eyes, the man said:"He's the connection to your past !!"

Chapter 2

Shocked as I hear that the old man say the person in the painting had a past connection with me

"How ??", I sounded clueless

"It all started with a glimpse of her ...", He said and started narrating their story

At the library when she was reading a book, completely focused in search of an answer to an ongoing battle in her mind as her thoughts screamed

"Hello !!", He said

She kept mum, unaware that everyone had left the library of the Hill House and she was left alone, she still kept mum turning the pages

"You there?", He again asked a little sharply that got her back into reality from her own little world of books and plays as she saw him a few seconds later and said

"Oh !! Hello !! I didn't realize you're calling me...I was completely focused on finding an answer from this book but still, I don't find it at all", She said to the young person who was standing right in front of her

"Relax, you'll get it soon .. probably I may help you out with it !!"..he said

"No, that's alright..!! I'll help myself"she said

"At this hour ...?? It's already 11 PM here !!", He said as he pointed the clock to me

"11 PM ?? What ??", She said shockingly as didn't realize the time

"Yes and it's been since morning you've been here", he said

"Oh !! No...I need to rush back home"

She quickly started packing her books in her bag and left the library back to her home

Back home, a thought that ran her nerve as she thought about him

He, A Calm and Composed person

A subtle smile that he wore always

Sharp yet polite tone

"Who is he ??", She thought smiling unusually,"Oh! Never mind, maybe he's someone who I've been knowing or never known ... or maybe I've seen him somewhere ... Anyways... let's sleep !!"

And the next day, she went to the library again

"Welcome Sir !!", Said the librarian to the prince who just enters the library a few minutes after she came

He sees the same girl whom he had spoken to last night in the library

She, Sweet and Innocent as she is

Deep bold eyes that allured deeply

Draped in peach

Focused mind on the book in search of an answer to an ongoing battle in her mind

"Sir, May I know who is seated at the corner table with a huge book? , The prince asked the librarian

"She, Oh !! She's Nell, She's a Writer, An Artist and just like you, She's an avid book reader, You'll always find her reading a lot of books, collecting stories the whole day !! After all, that's her task ...And yes !! She loves theatre as well !!"

"Theatre !! And How are you aware of it?"

"She comes here daily and reads books related to theatre, drama, fiction, poems, history, psychology... and her list is huge... Basically, she writes short stories, theatre plays and many of her plays have been acted by the actors .."

"Oh !! Interesting !!", He smiled and walked towards her where she is seated at the table at the corner of the library and sat in front of her

"Hello Nell !!", The prince said smilingly

She looked up at him, with a slight smile she said,"Hello !!"

He was the same person whom she had seen last night at the library

"I suppose you've met me last night when there was no one at the library"

"Yes,!! Exactly!!", The prince smiled

"I'm Neil, The Prince of the Hill House !! ..I just got to know from the librarian that you're a short story writer and you've written many theatre plays as well and I've seen them ... I mean... I just love them... every play has a meaning or a message to convey ...and look at me ...I can't even write one properly... Honestly,The amount of patience you have is just so amazing...I must say !!"

He continued..."Also, I may be good at Acting or portraying what's been told me to do but seriously not too good or very good at writing stories or plays ....So... Will you...."

Overwhelming as it seemed to Nell, she interrupted him..." Thank you so much, Sir, for the kind appreciation for the plays you've seen, I'd love to write more stories and theatre plays, Truly Sir ... Thank you so much", she said these words with a smile

"That's alright Nell, Please don't address me as Sir, I feel a bit weird, Since we both belong to the same field of arts and are almost of the same age group You can call me Neil"

"Surely Mr Neil, Honestly I strongly feel that everyone's got their own strengths and weaknesses and no one is perfect in any way, Also imperfections are good and it's completely alright to be imperfect.."

"Yes .. fact as this is ...So... Will you be here or Would you mind me walking in the woods"- Neil asked

"Sure ... Probably..let's walk in the woods and collect some stories .." - Nell said

They walked into the woods talking about their lives, childhood memories...etc ...and they walked till the lake ...

"The sun's setting...I must leave .." - Nell said to Neil as she sees the Sun setting

"I believe you're on the opposite side of the lake .." - Neil asked

"Yes, I do ...I'll cross the bridge and go home , I stay in a cottage , So , Would you come along ..." - Nell

"Yes definitely I'd love to but may not be today I believe you're getting late .." - Neil

"Yes !!"- Nell

They hugged each other and Neil waved her a goodbye

"Bye ...!! Take Care !!", Nell said this to Neil

Neil smiled as he heard these words from Nell and left the bridge for going home

From a far distance..they were being watched by someone whose devilish intentions are to ruin someone's life completely ,And Neil too could sense that he was being watched by someone whom he's never met or ever seen He too left that place and went back to the Hill House.

Chapter 3

"Neil met Nell ...No ...Never"

He thought with a lot of jealousy and hate in his mind and As he was watched Neil and Nell who just left the bridge after meeting each other

"Nell is mine", he said to himself and left the place where he usually makes paintings

He made many paintings of Nell but never spoke to her face to face as he stalked her quite often from a distant

"Those beautiful wavy locks suit you, Nell ...You're really beautiful my gorgeous girl, but the person with you, Ain't the right one...I could be the one for you but you may not accept me", He said this to himself as he saw the painting made of Nell

Nik, He's The Devil with an evil mind and devilish intention, and yet he could transform himself from devil to human at any point of time,

He Hypnotized people for his own benefit and sucked their blood completely till he made them energy less and old. Although he stayed miles away from the forest, people still feared him and about their own whereabouts

Days, Months and years passed on, Nell and Neil grew closer and closer as their relationship grew stronger. They lived a happy married life at the Hill House till an unexpected twist had turned their lives completely upside down

"Please let me in", He said to the gatekeeper

*Who are you? , I've not seen you before", said the gatekeeper

"I'm Mike Famous painter and artist I've been hired by Mr Neil for the Hill house" - Mike

"Sure you may proceed !!"- Gatekeeper

"Thank You !!"- Mike

As he walked towards the hill house from the gate, the roses started to wither away as he entered the hill house

He used the dark winding staircase to reach Neil's room

"Hello, Sir !!". Said, Mike

"Oh !! Mr Mike !!, It's a pleasure of you being here, please be seated here"- Neil

"Thank you Sir !!"- Mike

"Welcome to our Hill House and As you're aware that you've been hired as the painter and I have seen your paintings a lot in many exhibitions and I really appreciate the colours you have used and the themes you've painted, but I'd like to know who's that lady you've painted in the recent last exhibition I've seen which was 3 months ago"- Neil asked Mike

"She is my dream girl the one whom I desire for the most but never came into my life" - Mike

"Hahaha ...Oh !! So so you too you love fantasies and I'm sure she'll come into your life very soon" - Neil

"Definitely hoping for the right one to come in, So what would you like me to paint? Or you're particular about any certain theme ..like Nature, Indian style, Expression…." - Mike

"Umm...Well ..I'd prefer more into nature and portraits and definitely I love modern art as well which looks good when hung on the walls and of course, acrylic and oil paints is really something that I and my wife love the most, Come along, I'll show you"- Neil

They both go upstairs on the rooftop where the sunset can be seen and there's a small guest room and Neil opens the door

"So, Mike, from here, you can easily see the sunrise and the sunset and this place is quite peaceful to make the paintings, as you'd not be disturbed by anyone from the Hill House" - Neil

"Sounds Interesting Sir, I'd love to be in a peaceful place and make painting..as you know that, with a disturbed state of mind you literally can't make paintings peacefully and that's the reason why I stay miles away from the town area", Mike says this as he looks deeply in Neil's eye trying to hypnotize him but Neil diverts him saying

"So Mike, Basically, I want you to stay here as you can keep your belongings here and there are colours, canvas ... etc, all the things you require are here, if there's anything you require please don't hesitate, feel free" - Neil

"Neil... Neil...Neil...Where are you ?" - Nell

Nell comes to the entrance of the guest room where Neil and Mike are

"Honey, where have you been? , I've been searching for you in the whole house?"- Nell

"And"- Neil

"And, you're busy here !!"- Nell

"Well we're supposed to go for dinner tonight !!", She continued

"My gorgeous darling, we're definitely going for dinner tonight but let me tell you the artist whom we've hired is here .."- Neil

"Oh !! I see !!"- Nell

"So I was showing him the guest room where he can peacefully make paintings, Also so he doesn't take much time to paint probably 10 minutes or so"- Neil

"Well !!, Sir sorry to interrupt but I can make it within 10 minutes as well"- Mike

"Oh !! Really !! That's amazing then why don't you make a painting of Nell"- Neil

"Now ??"- Nell

"Yes !!"- Neil

"Sure, I'll be back in few minutes ready"- Nell

"By then, I'll set up my canvas"- Mike

15 minutes later, Nell comes back dressed up in a red gown seated on a chaise lounge sofa to the guest room where Mike does his paintings on the rooftop of the Hill house

"Can you make a painting of me and Neil together?"- Nell

"Sure Ma'am"- Mike

Neil stood beside Nell and Mike started making the painting of them, Although he wasn't ready to make one for both of them

At the end, Mike made their painting

"Sir, The painting is ready"- Mike

"Oh! Can we have a look at it"- Neil

"Sure Sir"- Mike

"Come Nell"- Neil

Neil and Nell see their painting being made on the canvas

"Wow !! What a Masterpiece it is !! I really appreciate it"- Neil

"I look more beautiful in this painting and It's amazing"- Nell

"My love, You're very beautiful be it a painting or in reality", saying this to Nell, Neil Kissed her forehead

"Thank You, Love !!"

"Well !! Can we hang this in our room?"- Nell asked Mike

"Sure Ma'am, It's yours and Sir's"- Mike

"So can we leave for dinner?"- Neil

"Sure, We can !!"- Nell

Neil and Nell left the guest room with their painting to their room and then left the Hill House for the dinner quite happily

Meanwhile, at the Guest Room of the Hill House, He stood at the mirror and said to himself

"You seriously made their painting? Instead of yourself and Nell ??"

Strange as though it seems, He could see himself as the Vampire and not the Human

"Nik ...", He said

"Oh No !! Mike !!... You're the Human ?", and starts laughing devilishly

"Nik...Mike...Mike...Nik...Nik...Mike...Mike...Nik... Nike...Mike...Noo...!!! None of them...But How about being Neil forever and getting closer to Nell ? .."

"Yes ..!! That'd be much better ..Nell is Mine ..You hear me, Neil ...She's never yours"...He Continued

"I heard you Nik .." - Neil said this as he comes into the guest room where Nik stays

"And I've seen your devilish side as well, I'm shocked to see that you're a Vampire but not a Human"- Neil continued

Unaware of being overheard and watched, Nik turns around and says

"Damn it, Neil !!, You get me wrong !! I'm a Human !! I'm Mike and You've hired me as an Artist"- Nik

"Whether you're Mike or Nik ...you're the Devil and you don't deserve to be here in my house ...Go Away you Devil !!"- Neil

"WOW !! Isn't it amazing Mr Neil !! You've approached the devil yourself and now you're saying it to go away ??, You've invited the devil yourself after seeing the painting and Now...You're asking me to leave? HOW?"

Nik paused for a moment, then he continued

"I ask you ..HOW ?? ...Aren't you aware that my paintings are very Hypnotizing...They attract everyone to it and the colours I use catches attention within seconds and I use the same colours everywhere...So, You and Nell are under my control ...Don't you know that Devil's more stronger than a Human ?? and you can't control the Devil ...So I say ...Go and Kill Nell"- Nik says this in a very commanding manner and is frustrated with the fact that Neil and Nell are together

"No...I won't !! She's the love of my life and she'll be with me forever and throughout my lifetime, And Neither will you harm me nor will you even go closer to her"- Neil says this as he's completely frustrated and realized that Mike had cheated on him

"I'd never know that you would actually take help from a vampire and were continuously transforming yourself from a human again and again to fulfil the desire of being a famous artist and gain fame" - Nik says further

Neil takes out a gun and tries shooting the Devil, he continues"Go away, you devil ...You don't deserve to be here among us"

"Don't forget that you're trying to shoot the devil and the devil doesn't die"- Nik

Saying this in a very devilish way, Nik Hypnotizes Neil in such a way that he falls unconscious and dead on the floor.

Chapter 4

"Oh !! damn !! Poor Nell !! She might be waiting for Neil...But Nik's really devilish ..he killed him ...How can he be so Inhuman and Ruthless? - Shia asked the Old man

"Then what happened ?.." She questioned him

The old man continues

Nik transformed himself as Neil and kept everyone under his control

Day by Day, One by One ..people started going missing or dying due to certain health issues in the Hill House ..Trees, Plants ..started withering ..and Seeing all this happen, Nell Couldn't tolerate this

She started missing those old days where she used to enjoy herself in the rose garden along with Neil

She could sense that Neil was being murdered ruthless and decides to leave the Hill House...But Nik stops her

"Nell, Don't leave me ..I'm your forever love" - Nik

"My love and you...No ways !! you aren't the same person when I met and married you...You've changed a lot these days...I feel you're more disguised ..you ain't Neil but someone else ..whom I hate the most ..Whom I feared the most"- Nell

"You ain't that person anymore ...whenever I'm around you or when you're around me...I feel uncomfortable, unloved ..unattentive...I feel as if I hate myself...I feel pain when you're around me...You aren't Neil but someone in his form...Tell me who you are", Nell cried out her feelings

"Honey, I'm Neil, your love and I still love you just the way I did when I married you ..These tears get me into pain ...Please don't cry"- Nik

"Don't try to influence me or hypnotize me with your words ..these don't work out with me ...You can't see what's happening around ??, Each and everyday people missing or dying or suicides that are happening at the Hill House...My rose garden has completely withered away .trees and plants have completely lost their lives...A lot of things have Shattered these days and you're still ignoring these ??"

Nik Keeps Mum...

"You aren't the same person whom I'd known from years, You've changed ..and You aren't my love anymore"- Nell Continued

Nik couldn't control his anger anymore, Out of anger, he said to Nell

"I've been telling you a hundred times that I'm your love and I'm not disguised person, But I believe that you lack trust in me? , I understand that people are going missing and suicides are happening day by day ..." - Nik

"And you're still calm;" - Nell interrupted

"And again you're still calm, you're just living as though nothing has ever happened...How can you tolerate this ???, Yes, I don't trust you anymore and you don't even deserve it as well

Saying this in the angry tone, Nell goes back to her room from the rooftop of the Hill House

"I must plan something", Nik thought after Nell left the rooftop

A few hours later, In the late evening, Nik goes to Nell's room and finds her seated on her sofa reading a book, He goes close to her and says,"Honey, Let's go out for dinner !!"

"No, I'm not interested"- Nell

"Oh! Come on Nell !! It's been very long since we've gone out together anywhere and you seem to be depressed a lot ..Come On...Let's go"- Nik

Nell doesn't pay attention to Niks words and continues to read her book

"Nell, Let's go out !!" - Nik

She continues to ignore him

"Nell ..." - Nik

Nell gives a deep side look into Nik's eye and says, "Yes Nik ..tell me that you're not Neil anymore"

Her words were a shock to Nik, "How did she even get to know my real identity?", Nik thought

"Nell, I'm Neil, I'm your husband and Who's Nik ?"- Nik

"Nik's a Devil, Neil's a Human, Nik can disguise himself into anyone to gain anything he desires, it could be a human or plainly anything. He even practices wit craft, black magic, hypnosis, Faking himself to be an artist he actually took people's lives by hypnotizing them and making paintings through their blood that he sucked"- Nell

"What are you saying Nell, Have you ...??" - Nik

"I've seen you painting on a canvas and invoking the devilish energy at the same time and you don't use red colour but you use someone's blood and you combine blood with the rest of the other colours which create a very unique colour and these colours have been used in all your paintings, I've seen until today and that's how you've made money. To this extent you even made my painting with these colours and tried getting closer to me, Until today, you've never spoken to me face to face and used this method to get closer to me ?? Is this the truth ??"- Nell

"Nell .." - Nik

"No, This is the truth, all these days you've been faking as Neil but actually you murdered him that night itself when me and Neil had come back from the dinner... Why have you done this Nik? Why? Just to get closer to me ??"- Nell

Nik kept mum for a minute

"I need an Answer Nik !! ..." - Nell

Nik gives a devilish smile and says,"Oh poor girl !! Poor chap !! Yes !! I'm Nik, The devil and I've murdered Neil for my own benefit and that's just to get closer to you ...yeah !! I've never spoken to you before but I was a hell jealous when you met Neil and I was desiring for you always, I made a lot of attempts to speak to you those days back in college and I tried impressing you a lot but you were never impressed by me", Saying these words Nik twists Nell's Hand

"Stop It Nik ...You're hurting me"- Nell

"No ...I'm not ...I'm not hurting you...But you've hurt me a lot ....since then ...You slowly became a famous story writer and left me behind unaware that I too wanted to be one .." and pushed Nell towards the window

"Please leave me ...Please ..." - Nell

"The devil never spares anyone's life it has been ruined because of ...It never lets anyone go off...the devil's always thirsty for blood and it wanted yours as well but never got it"- Nik

"No ...Please ...I beg you ...Please ..." - Nell

"Poor Chap"- Nik

"Nik, what do you desire ?"- Nell

"Me.??... I desire you only !!"- Nik says and turns towards the entrance of the room

"Alright", Nell said this and reaches out for a hunter weapon that was placed in the drawer next to the window

"Go away you Devil"- She said this and stabs Nik from the Back

Nik falls unconscious and Nell runs away from there. She ran as fast as she could towards the entrance of the Hill House and the doors closes by itself

Chapter 5

"Open the door...Please ..Someone...Please help me ..I need to get out of this place", Nell starts banging the door

"Open it ..." Nell shouts for help

"That door will not Open poor chap", Nik says this in a devilish tone.

Shocked to hear him back, Nell turned around and said"But I just killed you"

"No Human can kill The Devil.." - Nik

"Nik...Please leave me,..I beg you ..I've never harmed you...Please leave me .." Nell cries out

"No ..My gorgeous baby !!... Now, I'll not spare you, sweety .." - Nik says this as he gets closer to Nell

"You've made me suffer and now it's my turn to make you one ...", He says this and starts to look deeply into Nell's eye

He hypnotizes her and kills her

"later On..." - The Old man said ...

"Then what Happened ...??"Shia

"Where am I ?", Shia said this to herself as she wakes up to a weird place

"Hello !! Is anyone here??", She asked...

"Don't worry, I'm here for you", A person's voice said these words to her

"But I can't see you, Who are you? , What do you want from me ?" - Shia

"I'm Neil, I know you can't see me but can hear me... It's for two days you're lying here unconscious"- Neil

"2 days ??" - Shia asked Neil

"How ??" - She continued

"The person who was telling you about my past is none other than Nik himself who murdered me and you"- Neil

"Me??" - Shia

"Yes, you were Nell before, 25 years ago, I witnessed you being hypnotized and murdered ruthlessly by him,...But I'm sorry that I couldn't save you and Today he's targeting you again"- Neil

"So, you mean to say that Nik is still alive and practicing hypnosis and black magic?"- Shia

"Yes, it is ...he..." - Neil

"But he's a Devil and we can't kill him"- Shia

"He's grown old ..I'm sure his powers might have doubled?"- Shia continued

"No, It has not ..since 25 years after Nell's death he lost half of his powers and became more of a cursed person. He tried regaining his powers back but He failed ..he cannot

transform himself much but can hypnotize people which doesn't last for long as he thinks .." - Neil

"Then ??"- Shia

"The only way out is ..." - Neil

"Good Morning Girl !! I'm glad that you've woken up after 2 long days of sleep ..you were so interested in the story that you slept deeply"- Nik

"Hmm..." - Shia

"Anyways, I've got you a pie to eat...Please do have it...It's delicious ..and your favorite too ..Apple pie .." - Nik

Neil senses that the pie in Nik's hand is spelled with poison and tried to stop Shia from having it

"Thank You !! But I don't have pie"- Shia

"I've especially made this for you dear...Please have it .." - Nik

"I'm by no way or any way related to you and I dislike pies...Thanks anyway ..!! , I need to leave .." - Shia

"But where ??"- Nik

Shia gets up and leaves to the Hill House where she finds out the actual truth about Nik which will be hidden in a corner of the room at the Rooftop of the Hill House

"So this is it !!"- Shia

"HaHaHa...So you thought you'll kill me"

She heard a person behind her and turns around, Shocked to see Nik right behind her

"Yes, I'm the Devil and Murdered a lot of people, even Neil and Nell and ended their story as well ..I was the one who disguised as Neil and stayed with Nell just to get closer to her ..I use blood as my colors and hypnotized people and Now It's your turn for me to hypnotize you and take your blood young lady !!" - Nik

He smiled devilishly as he said these words to Shia

"You can't do anything to me Nik"- Shia

She pauses for a moment and looks deeply into Nik's eye and stabs him right away in his chest and Nik falls down completely dead and starts burning into flames.

Shia leaves the Hill House quickly saving herself from the fire and starts running as fast as she could. Finally she came to the entrance of the bridge where Neil was waiting for her

"Neil, You're here !!"- Shia

"Yes !!"- Neil

"My time is nearing ..I need to leave"- Neil continued

"But why ??"- Shia

"I'm Set free, completely awake for a new journey... Thank you ....Thank you so much, Shia, for setting me free from this devil, you're truly my love ..I wish you all the good luck and happiness and I hope you become a Famous writer and live a very Happy Life...Good Bye and God Bless !!"- Neil

Saying these words to Shia , Neil disappears in the white light for a new journey

"Shia...Shia ....Where have you been ?? Are you Alright ??" - Ron says this as he comes running to Shia

"Hey !! Ron !! I'm Alright ..I Just got lost and ..." - Shia

"And what about the mystery of the Hill House you were searching for everywhere ??"- Ron

"Sorted"- Shia

"What ??"- Ron

"Oh Nevermind.!! Let's go camping !!"- Shia

And they left the place

*************THE END ************

www.ingramcontent.com/pod-product-compliance
Lightning Source LLC
LaVergne TN
LVHW050428160726
843469LV00041B/1281